WOLF

KILLER KING OF THE FOREST

ANGELA ROYSTON

WINDMILL
BOOKS™

New York

Published in 2014 by Windmill Books, An Imprint of Rosen Publishing
29 East 21st Street, New York, NY 10010

Produced for Windmill by Calcium Creative Ltd
Editor for Calcium Creative Ltd: Sarah Eason
US Editor: Sara Howell
Designers: Paul Myerscough and Keith Williams

Photo credits: Dreamstime: Albertoloyo 26, Genlady 27b, Mirceax 25b,
Plumkrazy 27t, Marcel Schauer 28, Twildlife 24, Wollwerth 29; Shutterstock:
AISPIX by Image Source 9b, Thomas Barrat 23, S Belov cover, 10, Volodymyr
Burdiak 7b, creativex 8, 9t, jo Crebbin 5l, s-eyerkaufer 18, Gemenacom 16,
Arto Hakola 25t, keeskoopmans 7t, KKulikov 15, kochanowski 17b, Eirikur
Kristjansson 17t, m6photo 11, melis 6, NancyS 14, outdoorsman 19t, Denis
Pepin 1, 12, Pi-Lens 22, Scott E Read 19b, George Spade 5r, Stayer 4, 20,
Debbie Steinhausser 13t, Vishnevskiy Vasily 13b, visceralimage 21.

Library of Congress Cataloging-in-Publication Data

Royston, Angela, 1945–
 Wolf : killer king of the forest / by Angela Royston.
    pages cm. — (Top of the food chain)
 Includes index.
 ISBN 978-1-61533-738-5 — ISBN 978-1-61533-793-4 (pbk.) —
 ISBN 978-1-61533-794-1
 1. Wolves—Juvenile literature. 2. Predatory animals—Juvenile literature. I.
 Title.
 QL737.C22R686 2014
 599.773—dc23

                              2013002095

Manufactured in the United States of America

CPSIA Compliance Information: Batch #BS13WM: For Further Information contact Windmill Books, New York, New York at 1-866-478-0556

CONTENTS

Forest King 4

Meet the Wolves 6

Top Predator 8

Wolf Senses 10

Wolf Fur 12

Stalking Prey 14

Wolf Attack 16

Pack Life 18

Wolf Talk 20

Making a Mark 22

Competition 24

Wolf Dangers 26

No More Wolves? 28

Glossary 30

Further Reading and Websites ... 31

Index 32

FOREST KING

Wolves are king in the huge **coniferous** forests that stretch across northern Canada, Alaska, northern Europe, and Siberia. Their howls echo through the pine and fir forests in these places. Wolves live farther south, too, in **deciduous** forests and the grasslands around them.

Wolves **prey** on elk, moose, and other animals that live in the forests. The animals they prey on feed on plants, such as shrubs, grass, moss, and pinecones. The wolves, moose, and plants form a **food chain**. Wolves are at the top of the chain and the plants, which make their own food from sunlight, are at the bottom of the food chain.

*Wolves usually hunt in pairs, or in a larger group of wolves, called a **pack**.*

Elk are one of the main animals eaten by wolves.

Most wolves live in the taiga. This is a huge area of pine and fir forests, south of the Arctic Circle.

KILLER FACT

Wolves live in different areas of the world. They are found in the icy Arctic, but they also live in the hot deserts of the Middle East. Wolves once lived almost everywhere on land, but now they are most common in very wild places.

5

MEET THE WOLVES

Wolves belong to the dog family, which also includes wild dogs, coyotes, jackals, and foxes. All pet dogs are thought to have come from wolves. German shepherd dogs and huskies still look like wolves, but most pet dogs now look very different from wolves.

Gray wolves or timber wolves have gray, brown, and black fur. Arctic wolves live north of the forests in North America and Greenland. They are colored white, which **camouflages** them against the snow that covers the ground in these places for most of the year. Smaller wolves also survive farther south, such as in the Rocky Mountains. Ethiopian wolves, for example, live in the mountains in Ethiopia in Africa.

Huskies live happily in the snow and are often used to pull sleds.

Lemmings are always on the lookout for their enemy, the wolf.

Links in the Food Chain

Arctic wolves prey mostly on caribou, musk oxen, and Arctic hares. They also snack on smaller animals, such as lemmings, and may even catch seals and birds, such as ptarmigan. They eat all of their prey, even the bones!

The gray wolf has patches of white fur, which help to camouflage it against the patchy snow where it lives.

7

Wolves are designed to be a top **predator**. They have sharp senses, and their bodies are **streamlined** and well camouflaged. They have powerful muscles, strong backs, and can run very quickly. They can also keep running for a long time, which allows them to chase prey until it is tired. Then the wolves pounce on the victim!

A wolf keeps its head low and level with its shoulders as it runs. This streamlined shape allows the animal to move fast and its large paws can grip onto different types of ground. Wolves have bristly hairs between their toes, which helps them move across the snow. Their blunt claws can also grip onto slippery rocks.

A wolf uses its strong sense of smell, its hearing, and its eyesight as it stalks its prey.

Packs of wolves watch their prey together. The pack tries to pick out a weak animal to attack.

KILLER FACT

Wolves can run for hours at 5 to 10 miles per hour (8–16 km/h) which helps them cover large areas while looking for prey. They can burst into a terrifying speed of up to 35 miles per hour (56 km/h) to bring down prey.

With its head bent low, a wolf can run quickly across the snow.

9

WOLF SENSES

Of all their incredible **senses**, wolves use their amazing senses of smell and hearing the most. Their sense of smell is 100 times better than a human's and they can pick up smells that are more than 1 mile (1.6 km) away! Wolves can hear even better than dogs and can hear sounds that are up to 10 miles (16 km) away.

Although wolves cannot see things that are far away, they see well over short distances. They usually hunt in the dark and see better at night than during the day. Wolves have one more big advantage over their prey. They are smarter than most of the animals they hunt!

Light reflects off the back of a wolf's eyes to help it see better in the dark.

As wolves run, they listen out for the sounds of other wolves as well as those of prey.

Links in the Food Chain

Wolves use their intelligence to help them find food. Early settlers in North America noticed that wolves often followed them as they hunted. The wolves hung back until a bison was killed, then moved in to snatch a free meal.

WOLF FUR

A wolf's fur keeps it warm and blends in with the wolf's **habitat**. Northern wolves, which live in the coldest places, have two layers of fur. A thick, fluffy undercoat keeps the wolf warm in winter. On top of the undercoat is an outer layer of long hairs. Snow and water slide off the long hairs to protect the undercoat beneath.

Gray wolves have gray-brown fur with light and dark patches. The colors camouflage the wolves against rocks and trees. Wolves that live deep in the forest are almost black to match their dark surroundings. Arctic wolves are white so they can hide against the snow.

An Arctic wolf's thick white fur keeps it warm and camouflages it against the snow and ice.

This gray wolf's fur is similar in color to the tree trunks and soil where it lives.

KILLER FACT

Wolves are so well **insulated** by their fur, they survive through winter without a den. They just curl up on the snow, put their noses between their back legs, and cover their faces with their bushy tails. Their ears remain pricked, however, alert for sounds of danger or of prey.

This wolf looks as if it is fast asleep, but its ears are pricked to catch any sounds.

Wolves hunt mostly at night, from dusk onward. They use their sense of smell to find their prey. When the wolves pick up the scent of the prey, they track it. They try to creep up to a herd of animals without being spotted.

The wolves then try to separate the weakest animals from the rest of the herd. These are creatures that are young, old, injured, or sick. This usually makes them easier to kill. Sometimes a herd of large animals, such as musk oxen, stand their ground and protect the weaker animals. If this happens, the wolves often give up the hunt.

Wolves hide among trees as they stalk prey through the forest.

Reindeer fawns often keep watch in opposite directions to look out for wolves that might try to attack them.

Links in the Food Chain

In Minnesota, gray wolves prey mostly on whitetail deer, but they also catch moose, beavers, and snowshoe hares. Wolves kill only as many animals as they need to survive. In Minnesota it is estimated that about 3,000 wolves kill about 50,000 deer a year. That's about the same number of deer as human hunters kill.

15

WOLF ATTACK

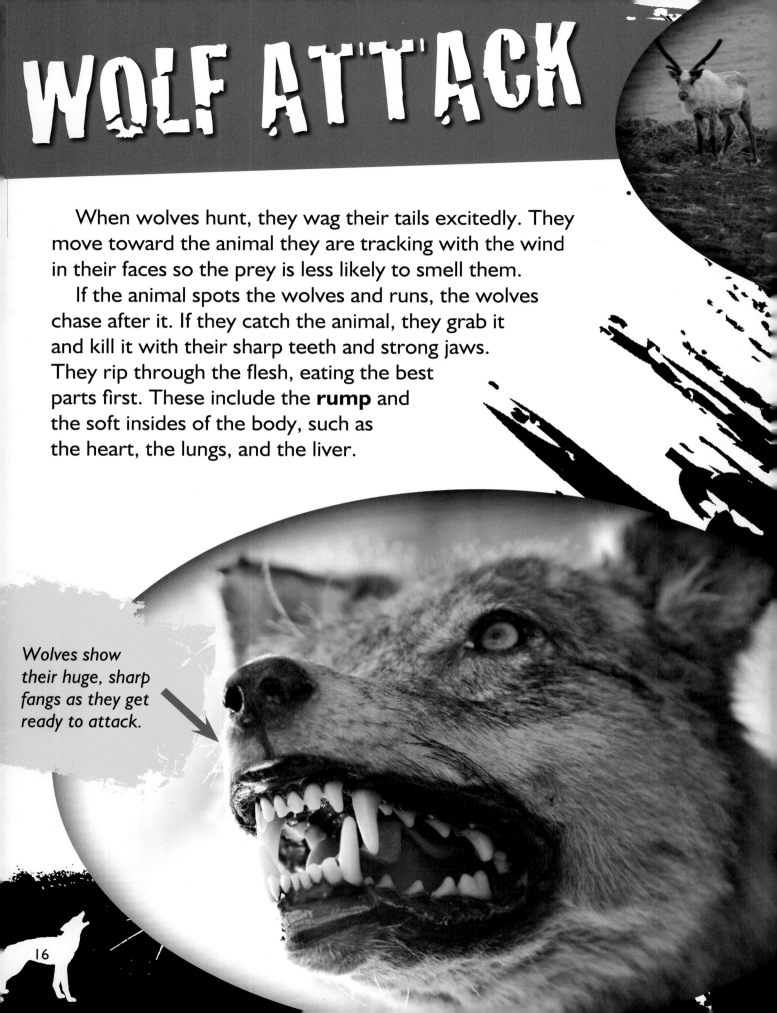

When wolves hunt, they wag their tails excitedly. They move toward the animal they are tracking with the wind in their faces so the prey is less likely to smell them.

If the animal spots the wolves and runs, the wolves chase after it. If they catch the animal, they grab it and kill it with their sharp teeth and strong jaws. They rip through the flesh, eating the best parts first. These include the **rump** and the soft insides of the body, such as the heart, the lungs, and the liver.

Wolves show their huge, sharp fangs as they get ready to attack.

Wolves often trap a herd of reindeer against the side of a lake. This stops the reindeer from running away.

Wolves hunt both large and small prey, including rabbits.

KILLER FACT

Each wolf needs 3–10 pounds (1.3–4.5 kg) of meat a day, but can eat up to 22 pounds (10 kg) in one sitting. A big meal will last a wolf for several days. Wolves eat quickly. They want to finish their meal before larger animals, such as grizzly bears, try to steal their kill.

PACK LIFE

Most wolves live together in packs of 8 to 15 wolves. Each pack includes a male, a female, and their offspring. Sometimes a male wolf will live on its own, as a lone wolf, until it finds a female to mate with. Then the male and female wolf begin a new pack.

Before a female wolf gives birth, she finds a den. She may use an old den, or may make a new one in a riverbank or between the rocks. When her pups are born, the whole pack looks after them for the first eight months, until the pups are old enough to hunt with the pack.

The male wolf here is the biggest wolf in the pack.

Links in the Food Chain

Wolf pups are not top predators. They are often preyed on by golden eagles, grizzly bears, and black bears. Bears may dig through the earth to reach the pups in their dens. Adult wolves try to protect the pups by distracting the bears.

Wolf cubs love to sneak out of their den to watch what is going on outside!

Hungry grizzly bears are a great threat to wolf cubs.

WOLF TALK

The sound of wolves howling can be heard for long distances. Wolves howl to call together members of their pack and to tell each other danger is nearby. Like dogs, wolves also bark, growl, and whine to talk to each other. They also use **body language** to send messages.

A wolf pack is **social** and very organized. Each member has a special **rank**. The strongest male and female wolf are at the top of the group and are known as "alpha wolves." Weak wolves are at the bottom of the pack. Wolves use body language to show their rank. A strong wolf holds its tail high, while a weaker wolf submits by crouching low or rolling onto its back.

When one wolf howls, other wolves join in! Wolves howl the most in winter.

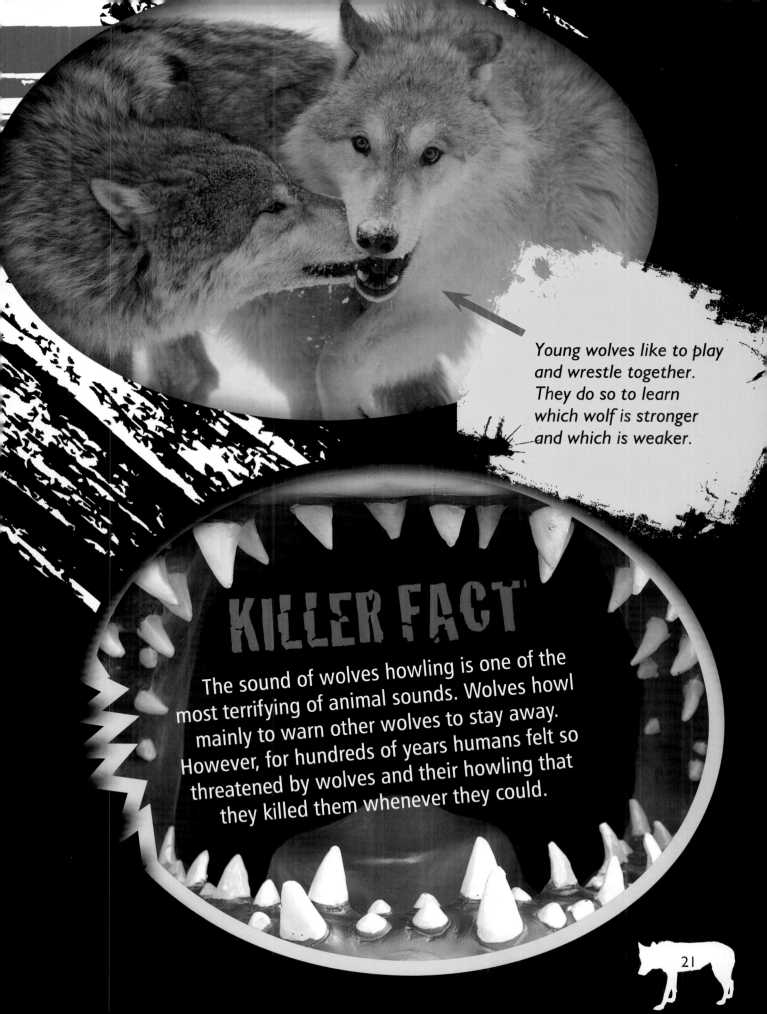

Young wolves like to play and wrestle together. They do so to learn which wolf is stronger and which is weaker.

KILLER FACT

The sound of wolves howling is one of the most terrifying of animal sounds. Wolves howl mainly to warn other wolves to stay away. However, for hundreds of years humans felt so threatened by wolves and their howling that they killed them whenever they could.

Smells are very important to wolves, especially their own smells. A wolf pack has its own **territory**, which it defends against other wolves. Wolves mark the edge of their territory with strong smells to warn other wolves to stay away.

Wolf smells are made by special **glands** at the top of the wolf's tail and in its paws. When a wolf urinates, it often scratches the ground afterward. The scratching probably gives off strong-smelling chemicals from the glands in the wolf's feet. Wolves mark their territory by urinating and by scratching tree trunks. Each wolf smells different, so members of the pack recognize each other by their smells.

These footprints were left by a wolf. Even if wolves cannot see another wolf's track, they can still smell it.

A wolf finds out about other wolves and possible prey by smelling the ground.

Links in the Food Chain

Although Ethiopian wolves live in packs that have their own territory, each wolf usually hunts alone. Ethiopian wolves feed mainly on rodents such as mole rats and grass rats. Sometimes the pack hunts together to chase and catch larger animals, such as antelope and lambs.

Wolves do not hold complete power at the top of their food chains. Wolves are **scavengers** as well as hunters. This means that they feed on dead animals when they can, and compete with other scavengers for food. Other scavengers include grizzly bears, coyotes, and cougars.

Bears and wolves prey on each other's cubs, and bears often try to drive wolves away from a recent kill so that they can eat it themselves. Wolves may try to steal a kill from a cougar. However, if the cougar fights back, it can injure or even kill a wolf. Wolves do not like coyotes either! Wolves drive them away and may kill coyotes that come onto their territory.

Cougars may look cute, but these animals are fierce fighters and will attack wolves to defend their young.

24

Links in the Food Chain

Many animals eat food left by wolves. Coyotes, foxes, and weasels quickly move in to feed on the remains of a wolf's meal. Ravens hang around while the wolves eat, waiting for leftovers.

Brown bears will chase away any nearby wolves to defend their cubs or their food.

Coyotes often wait for wolves to finish eating, so they can steal the remains of the wolves' meal.

WOLF DANGERS

Humans have always been the biggest threat to wolves. At one time, wolves were the most widespread mammals after humans. Since then, people have killed wolves, damaged their habitats, and killed their prey. Many wolves are now in danger of **extinction**.

Wolves have lost their prey because people shot the large animals, such as bison and moose, wolves preyed on. People also brought in cattle, sheep, and other farm animals to graze the land. Wolves soon realized that farm animals were easy prey, so farmers and hunters protected their animals by poisoning and shooting wolves.

There are fewer than 500 Ethiopian wolves still living in the wild. These are the most endangered of all wolves.

Links in the Food Chain

Arabian wolves live in a few scattered groups in the Middle East. They hunt hares, gazelles, and ibex, and scavenge whatever they can. They also attack small farm animals, such as lambs and goats. For this reason, farmers trap and kill wolves whenever they can.

Wolves are still hunted in Russia and in many other countries.

Wild red wolves became extinct in the wild in 1980. The wolves have since been bred in captivity and were released into North Carolina in 1987.

NO MORE WOLVES?

You might think that it would help animals such as deer and caribou if there were no wolves to prey on them. Scientists have found that this is not so. Food chains are complicated, and if just one animal in a food chain disappears, it has a big effect on all the other animals in the chain.

When wolves were released into Yellowstone National Park, scientists were surprised to find that the number of pronghorn antelope increased. Wolves prey on pronghorn, but coyotes prey on pronghorn fawns. The pronghorn benefitted because the wolves chased away the coyotes and more fawns were able to survive to become adults.

Gray wolves are now free to prowl in Yellowstone National Park.

Links in the Food Chain

Gray wolves prey on coyotes, as well as chase them off their territory. Coyotes prey on young pronghorn fawns and hunt small mammals such as prairie dogs, ground squirrels, and mice. These small animals eat plants and seeds.

Wolves may hunt pronghorn antelope, but the antelope do better alongside wolves because the wolves keep the food chain in balance.

GLOSSARY

body language (BAH-dee LANG-gwij) Using the position or movements of the body to send messages without speaking.

camouflages (KA-muh-flahj-ez) Makes something hard to see because its coloring blends into the surroundings.

coniferous (kah-NIH-fur-us) Made up of conifer trees. Conifer trees have needles instead of flat leaves and produce cones full of seeds.

deciduous (deh-SIH-joo-us) Trees with leaves that drop off, usually in fall.

extinction (ek-STINGK-shun) No longer in existence, having died out altogether.

food chain (FOOD CHAYN) Living things connected because they are one another's food.

glands (GLANDZ) Parts of the body that produce special chemicals.

habitat (HA-buh-tat) The natural environment in which a living thing is found.

insulated (IN-suh-layt-ed) Protected by a barrier from losing heat or becoming too hot.

pack (PAK) A group of wolves who live and hunt together.

predator (PREH-duh-ter) An animal that hunts other animals for food.

prey (PRAY) Animals that are hunted by other animals for food.

rank (RANK) The position that shows the level of importance in a group.

rump (RUMP) The buttocks, or fleshy parts of the back of a body, near the top of the tail.

scavengers (SKA-ven-jurz) Animals that feed on dead or rotting animals.

senses (SEN-sez) The parts of the body that detect particular things in the environment, such as light, chemicals, and sound waves. The senses give a living thing information about the world around it.

social (SOH-shul) Reacting with and communicating with other members of a group.

streamlined (STREEM-lynd) With a smooth, slim shape that moves easily through the air.

territory (TER-uh-tor-ee) An area of ground that a pack of wolves are prepared to defend against other wolves. Wolves will roam and hunt over a large area.

FURTHER READING

Brandenburg, Jim and Judy Brandenburg. *Face to Face with Wolves*. Face to Face with Animals. Des Moines, IA: National Geographic Children's Books, 2011.

Marsh, Laura. *Wolves*. National Geographic Readers. Des Moines, IA: National Geographic Children's Books, 2012.

Preszler, June. *Wolves*. World of Mammals. Mankato, MN: Capstone, 2006.

Simon, Seymour. *Wolves*. New York: HarperCollins, 2009.

Slade, Suzanne. *What if There Were No Gray Wolves?: A Book About the Temperate Forest Ecosystem*. Food Chain Reactions. Mankato, MN: Picture Window Books, 2011.

WEBSITES

For web resources related to the subject of this book, go to: www.windmillbooks.com/weblinks and select this book's title.

INDEX

A
Arabian wolves, 27
Arctic wolves, 5–7, 12

B
bears, 17, 19, 24–25
bison, 11, 26
body language, 20

C
camouflage, 6–8, 12
coniferous forests, 4
cougars, 24
coyotes, 6, 24–25, 28–29

D
deer, 15, 17, 28
den, 13, 18–19

E
elk, 4–5
Ethiopian wolves, 6, 23, 26

F
farmers, 26–27
food chains, 4, 7, 11, 15, 19,
    23–25, 27–29
foxes, 6, 25
fur, 6–7, 12–13

G
gray wolves, 6–7, 12–13, 15,
    28–29

H
howling, 4, 20–21

M
moose, 4, 15, 26
musk oxen, 7, 14

P
pronghorn antelope, 28–29

R
ravens, 25
red wolves, 27
running, 6, 8–11,16–17

S
scavengers, 11, 24, 27
senses, 8, 10–11, 13–14, 16, 20,
    22–23

T
teeth, 16
threats to wolves, 13, 21, 24–27
timber wolves, 6

W
wolf packs, 4, 9, 18, 20, 22–23